P9-DJA-418

The YARK

Bertrand Santini
illustrations by
Laurent Gapaillard

translated by
Antony Shugaar

GECKO PRESS

"One thing I have frequently observed in children, that when they have got possession of any poor creature, they are apt to use it ill."

—John Locke, 1693

1
THE
YARK

Of all the various Monsters that teem upon the face of the earth, the Human species is the most widespread.

There's another, though, more rare, less known.

It is the Yark.

The Yark loves children.

He loves the crackle of their little bones between his teeth, and to suck on their soft eyes, which melt like chocolate truffles.

He adores their tiny fingers, their tiny feet, their tiny tongues, which he chews with a sprig of mint for a sweet and deliciously sticky treat.

He is a discerning gourmet, who also enjoys sipping their brains, which—it seems—taste somewhat like marshmallow.

Without a shred of racist bias, he gobbles down children of every hue. Whatever their shade of brown, beige or pink, all children in the world have red blood and juicy hearts.

Beware of his jaws...

This mighty ogre has powerful fangs!

He glides silently over sleeping houses with the smell of fresh meat guiding him like a beacon through the night.

Listen closely!

He's turning the handle on your door...

And even if it's locked, his hooked nails are all he needs for keys.

Poor you! While you dream, he creeps up on velvet paws, careful not to make the floorboards creak. Looming over the bed, he leans in to sniff you.

Yum yum! Your almond and butter scent makes his mouth water...

His presence wakes you and you wonder: "Is it breakfast time already?"

That will be your last thought.

You blink your eyes, then open them wide. No! It's not a dream! He's here! Immense, like a black moon. Drool streams from his fangs as his jaws swing wide...

And that's that. It's over.

Without pain. Without a cry.

You've just been crunched up, under the helpless gaze of your terrified teddy bears.

The Yark also loves animals. But he considers them really too adorable to be gobbled up, so he never eats any.

2
THE WEAKNESS OF
MONSTERS

S till, beneath their ferocious appearance, Monsters always conceal some weakness that might ultimately lead to their ruin. King Kong was tender-hearted, Dracula was afraid of sunlight, the Colossus had feet of clay... As for the Yark, he has a delicate stomach.

This delicate stomach can tolerate only the flesh of very good children, in much the way that old people are able to digest only soup.

Numerous medical studies have shown that naughtiness modifies a child's chemical composition. When children do something wrong, their hearts ferment a violent poison and their flesh becomes more toxic than a viper's venom.

Listening only to his stomach, the Yark has occasionally eaten a bad child. But he soon regrets his indulgence. Liars give him heartburn, bullies and brats damage his teeth. As for little sadists, they tie his guts in knots.

Such a deplorable weakness of the digestive tract!

The Yark would a hundred times rather feast on bullies and spoiled kids, like a goat that chomps away happily while ridding the world of stinging nettles, weeds, and crabgrass.

But noble sentiments have never filled anyone's stomach. And certainly not a Monster's.

Nature, which has no moral code, is indifferent to matters of good and evil.

And since time out of mind, it's always been clear that the nicest are first to be eaten.

3
MODERN
CHILDREN

A h, how Monsters yearn for the good old days! Once upon a time, children were tender and innocent. Masquerading as a grandmother was enough to lure them within the swipe of a claw.

A steady diet of these little angels brimming with innocence ensured an iron constitution, year round.

Sadly, modern times have curbed the Yark's diet. Modern times produce practically no edible children.

These days, brats thrive on the earth like warts on a witch's chin. Schoolyards teem with brutish and nasty small persons who are the spitting image of their parents.

When still knee-high to a grasshopper, children already possess all the faults of adults. They play superheroes, boast and brag, but wet their pants the minute the hall light is switched off.

Garrulous, gluttonous, capricious, cowardly, good-for-nothing, lazy...truth be told, if they didn't make excellent stews, children would serve no purpose at all. Their primitive brains allow them to perform only the most rudimentary tasks. Eating, telling lies, and snickering is all they can accomplish in a day.

If only they had a shred of wit!

But resistant to deep thought or poetry, children of today laugh only at jokes about farts.

How long ago they now seem, those happy days when the Yark could gorge on vitamin-rich children. For the present day has adulterated not only the child's soul.

Laden with industrial products, the modern child has lost its nutritional value.

Its soft and flabby flesh now consists for the most part of cholesterol.

As for hygiene, *deplorable* is the word that leaps to mind. Children have become a hive of microbes, and prudence dictates that they be thoroughly boiled before serving at the table.

No, modern times are by no means easy for an ogre with a delicate stomach. And just as some species have fallen victim to the ravages of pollution, the loss of tender loving care and proper upbringings have pushed the Yark into the ranks of Monsters on the verge of extinction.

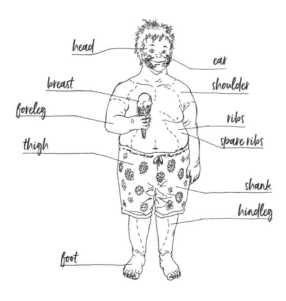

4
THE
LIST

Night has fallen. Like a tormented soul, the Yark wanders about in a forest buffeted by an icy wind. Exhausted, he seeks shelter.

Poor devil! Again tonight his empty stomach rumbles in despair.

No matter how long he spends hovering over schools, town squares, and orphanages, he catches only whiffs of indigestible brats.

"Where are edible children to be found?" the Monster laments. "There must be a few left somewhere!"

But in this world of scoundrels, it's like searching for a needle in a haystack!

One flake, then another… It's starting to snow. The Yark reckons he will certainly starve to death before Christmas.

As tears well up in his eyes, he suddenly lifts his head and cries out: "Santa Claus's list! Of course, that's the solution…"

This flash of genius makes him dance with joy.

"A feast! I just have to get my hands on that scrap of paper! That will give me the names and addresses of all the well-behaved children in the whole world! Ah, what a fool I've been! Why didn't I think of it sooner?"

Streamers of saliva drip from his chops as he thinks of that list, more enticing than a menu from the finest restaurant. And without a moment's delay, the Yark soars high into the sky, heading straight for Santa's home.

A few hours later, the Monster sets down near the North Pole. On the edge of a forest, he glimpses four twinkling dots of light: it's Santa Claus's house!

Knock! Knock! Knock!

"What's this? Who's visiting me so late?" the old man wonders.

When he opens the door of his cottage, Santa Claus comes face to face with a polar bear.

Of course, it's none other than the Yark! The sly devil has rolled in the snow to deceive this white-whiskered friend of children everywhere.

"Good evening, Santa Claus. I'm just a poor bear who's lost in the forest. May I come in to warm up?"

The good man welcomes his visitor with open arms.

"Come in, my friend! You're welcome in my home!"

The old man shuts the door and points his guest to a table decked with pastries smothered in whipped cream.

"You've come in the nick of time!" the kind man smiles. "We're about to serve dessert!"

"Yum... My mouth waters at the thought!" The Yark
salivates as his eye lights, not on the pastries, but on the
list of good boys and girls lying on a desk.

Cautiously, he sidles over. But as he edges past the fire-
place, the snow melts and the Yark's disguise vanishes

into a puddle. Santa recognizes the villain and his beard bristles like a big, angry cat.

"Get out of here, you foul beast! You child chomper!"

"A Monster has to eat!" the Yark retorts, quick as a flash.

"Sure, but not good little boys and girls! Do you want to put me out of a job?"

In one bound, the Monster lunges for the list before Santa can lift a finger. The old man fights back with the first weapon that comes to hand, a whipped cream dispenser.

"Back to Hades with you!" the old man shouts, strafing his visitor with powerful jets of cream.

The gooey geyser coats the Monster, turning him back into a polar bear. Blinded, he stumbles into a shelf, which collapses and buries the precious list under an avalanche of paper.

"The list! I can't find the list!" the Yark wails.

Foiled! Thwarted on the brink of victory!

The greasy Monster is forced to retreat into the black night without further ado.

When he runs out of breath and silence falls around him, the Yark bursts into sobs and flops down onto the snow.

"The list was my last best hope. This time, I'm done for!"

Just then, he feels something tickling his bottom. Reaching around and groping at his sticky back, his fingers pinch onto a piece of paper.

Surprised, he yanks at it. The paper comes away, tearing out a few hairs with it. The Yark stifles a cry of pain. But when he discovers in his hand the much-coveted list, his shout of victory echoes to the stars.

5

CHARLOTTE

The Yark hovers joyously. Above the seas, forests, and villages, his immense shadow looms over the sleeping world.

By the light of the moon, he feverishly skims through the list in search of the name of world's best-behaved girl. The description of a little girl named Charlotte, from Provence, in the south of France, whets his appetite: *Excellent pupil, impeccable hygiene, says prayers every night, clears the dinner table without being asked. P.S.: What's more, she sorts the recycling!*

"A culinary perfection!" the Yark cries in ecstasy.

It is true that those who top their class taste exquisite, reminiscent of the aroma of cherry pie.

In a frenzy of impatience, the Monster lets his full weight send him plummeting into the heart of Provence.

And now here he is. Already inside Charlotte's house.

On tiptoes, the ravenous visitor approaches her bed. His enormous bulk moves without a sound. As he gloats over his prey, a bouquet of aromas tickles his nostrils.

"Oh, yum!" purrs the Monster. "This good little girl smells absolutely scrumptious!"

Now he regrets not having brought accompaniments to round out his banquet. Because if green beans go with mutton the way mashed potatoes go with ham, nothing is more succulent than a leg of little girl garnished with a handful of peanuts.

His razor-sharp claw strokes the sleeping child's pink cheek.

"Hey there," he whispers, to wake her gently.

The one thing he mustn't do is frighten her! All good Monsters know that terror chills the blood and strips the flesh of its delicacy.

Charlotte opens her eyes. A shaggy mountain smiles down at her with all his jagged teeth.

"The Yark!" she shrieks.

But she adds a succession of senseless phrases: "Ah,

how wonderful! Thank you, Lord! The Yark has come!"

And Charlotte throws herself into the Monster's arms and showers him with kisses.

Flabbergasted, the Yark repels her with an indignant shove.

"But you should be afraid of me, silly girl! I'm a Monster!"

"Oh, but not just any Monster!" The girl smiles mischievously. "You're the Yark! And I read in a book that you can't eat naughty children."

"Oh, really? Hmm... That may be..." mutters the Yark, embarrassed to have his personal difficulties brought up like this. "But you're so nice, you're going to make a delicious meal," he continues in his big voice.

"Precisely," whispers the paragon of good conduct. "I'm sick and tired of being a good example! I badly want to misbehave... Only I never dare!"

There's a strange gleam in her eyes.

"But tonight, thanks to you, I'm going to have to!"

"What are you talking about?" asks the Monster, vaguely uneasy.

Whereupon Charlotte takes a small book from the drawer of her bedside table.

"This very instructive volume offers a thousand and one ways to defend oneself against Monsters. Several chapters are devoted to you..."

She leafs through a few pages, then reads a passage aloud:

In case of Yark attack, it is imperative that you immediately start misbehaving in order to make yourself inedible. If you do so, this Monster, which is allergic to bad children, will be unable to gobble you up. A swear word, a bare-faced lie, or pouring milk over your little brother will make you toxic for several hours. And if you pee on a carpet, you will remain inedible until daybreak.

"Shut up, shut up!" shrieks the Yark in a fit of rage. "That book doesn't know what it's talking about!"

But in fact the Monster's fury confirms that all this is true.

"All right then, let's see!" Charlotte says in triumph. "Where shall I start? Shall I say some swear words, pee on the floor, or murder my dolls?"

"No! Have mercy!" begs the Monster, down on his knees. "I'm so hungry! Don't make yourself inedible!"

Charlotte shuts the book with a determined look.

"I'm going to start with the swear words."

"You're too well mannered! You'll never be able to do it!" the Monster roars, beside himself.

"Poo! Pee! Fart!" the little girl bawls defiantly.

"My meal is ruined!" the Yark chokes between sobs.

The frenzied child leaps onto a table to chant this deplorable refrain: "With every fart, my Granny lets...her false teeth clack like castanets! Olé!"

"All that delicious food, gone to waste!" the Monster moans through his tears.

Drunk with delight, Charlotte races to the four corners of the room, tipping over furniture, ripping the hair from her dolls, stamping her teddy bears underfoot.

"What fun!" she whoops, pulling down her pajamas with the intention of taking a poop in her bookbag.

"No, no! Not that!" the Yark yells, indignant.

Suddenly, a commotion from the hallway interrupts their dispute. Alerted by Charlotte's cries, her father and mother have woken up.

"Your parents!" the Yark cries. "Ah, when they see this carnage, they'll give you a well-deserved spanking!"

"No, they won't! I'll tell them that you attacked me!"

"Oh, you will, will you? And how will you prove you're telling the truth?"

"With this!" Charlotte yanks a handful of hair from the Yark's bottom.

"Ouch!" shrieks the scandalized Monster. There really is nothing more sadistic on this earth than a well-brought-up little girl!

With a crash of breaking glass, he hurls himself through the window that he unfortunately doesn't have time to open.

The shock is such that a section of wall collapses.

At that moment, the girl's parents burst into the devastated room.

"What's going on?" asks her panic-stricken mother.

A first-rate actress, Charlotte melts into tears and throws herself into her father's arms.

"The Yark! He attacked me!"

"The Yark?" Her parents shudder.

"Yes! And I was forced to misbehave frightfully, to keep him from devouring me!"

"My poor darling!" Her mother moans and pulls the child to her.

Her father gravely examines a hank of hair lying on the floor.

"This is Yark hair, without a doubt!"

"You won't punish me will you, Papa?" Charlotte begs, turning her great doe eyes in his direction.

"No, my daughter. You did the right thing! And rest assured! After this fine lesson, that infamous Monster won't be back to bother you again!"

"You think not? Charlotte murmurs sadly, looking out at the stars through the devastated wall.

6

LEWIS

orrid, horrid, horrid girl!" the Yark thunders as he zigzags through a sky crisscrossed with lightning. Furious at his misadventure, he scratches out Charlotte's name with great scrawling Xs.

"Next!" he mutters.

For a hungry stomach never gives up, and the Yark has already singled out his next meal. This boy called Lewis lives in an old suburb of London.

"Sweet! An English child!" The Yark is delighted. He dotes on those little creatures, with their clear complexions, red hair, and hamster teeth.

With gaping maw and flapping tongue, the Monster plunges straight down toward English soil.

As he lands in front of Lewis's house, the Yark vows not to engage in a word of conversation.

No! This time there'll be no knock-knock at the door or how's it going, blah blah. He'll rear up like a demon in the bedroom, stride across the floor straight for the bed and lunge at the child. Unseen, unheard, he'll crunch him up raw.

Arriving at Lewis's bedroom, the Yark takes a deep breath. "No knocking at the door, no how's it going blah blah..." he tells himself again, to bolster his nerve. "Now go!"

The Yark rears up like a demon in the bedroom, strides across the floor, straight for the bed, and lunges at the child...

But horrors! The bed is empty!

"How can it be?" In a panic, the Monster rummages at the covers. At this hour, all good childen are snuggled under their covers! Where the dickens is that Lewis?

He bends over and takes a look under the bed...

There's no one...

A smell, however, tickles his nostrils. A whiff of little boy wafts around him. He sniffs again... His powerful nose distinguishes the scents of little eyes, little fingers, little feet, a little liver, and even, sniffing again, the bloody smell of a little heart hammering inside a little chest.

Suddenly, the Yark sees movement.

There!

In the blanket tent set up beside the bed.

Slowly, silently, the Yark opens the flap...

Inside, a little boy is staring him right in the eye.

"Who are you?" asks the kid, without a hint of fear.

Such coolness astonishes the Monster. Still, at least he hasn't been recognized. This child won't erupt into bad

language or take a poop in his bookbag to make himself inedible.

"And what are you doing here?" the small child insists.

"Whatever you do, don't answer!" the Yark tells himself, biting his cheeks. "Don't let yourself be bamboozled or weakened!" He's actually a softie, the Yark! How many times, because he stopped to chat with his prey, has he been stirred by pity as he munches? It's no fun hunting for your food, let alone feeling sympathy for the meal!

Killing a fellow creature is a rotten job and no Monster finds joy in these carnivorous crimes, with the exception, of course, of vampires, zombies, and toreadors.

"What's your name?" the child asks in an innocent tone.

But now, without standing on ceremony, the Yark opens his powerful jaws lined with sharp teeth and, snap! the little Englishman disappears down the gaping maw.

"Hurray! Tra-la-la-la-la!" the Monster whoops as he takes an elegant dance step or two. That little Lewis really was a scrumptious morsel!

He starts laughing and wiggles his hips.

"Ah, how delicious! Oh, what a feast! Ah, how nice to have a full belly!

But all at once, the Yark freezes. Sobs sound in the darkness. He pricks his ears... The sounds are coming from the wardrobe...

"Is someone in there?" the Monster whispers as he creeps over.

"Yes! For pity's sake let me out," begs a childish voice.

"And who are you?" the Yark demands.

The small voice responds with these two tragic words: "I'm Lewis!"

7

JACK

ewis? What do you mean, Lewis? The Monster fiddles nervously with the key to the cupboard, then with a sharp yank, pulls on the handle. The little boy who springs from the wardrobe throws himself into his rescuer's arms.

"Phew! Thanks! I was about to suffocate!"

"But who locked you in there?"

"My brother."

"Which brother?"

"Jack! My very bad big brother!"

"Very bad?" the Monster stammers, increasingly uneasy. "What do you mean by very bad?"

"He's a louse! A rat! He's the scummiest scumbag in

England! Every night he locks me in the wardrobe so he can play with my toys!"

At this point, the Yark realizes his terrible blunder.

"Ye gods! I've just eaten a scoundrel!"

"You ate Jack?" Lewis asks, incredulous.

"By mistake!" the Monster yelps. "It was a dreadful misunderstanding! It was you I was meant to eat! Now, I'm going to be sick! I'm allergic to brats and bullies!"

The truth is, the Yark already feels ill. His legs are trembling, his stomach is gurgling, his ears are buzzing, and his buttocks are starting to itch. He coughs, he drools, he suffocates, he breaks out in pimples, pustules, and blisters.

Without warning, he lets out a thunderous, flaming fart.

The fireball blasts through the room and chars Santa Claus's list into a shower of sparks.

"My list!" yells the Yark.

"Poor Monster!" sobs Lewis. "None of this would have happened if you'd gobbled me up instead!"

The Yark thinks that this child surely has a good heart, and he'd love to have eaten him with a little butter. But there's no time to daydream. Driven by a natural need, the Monster hurls himself out through the window once more and bounds off like a gazelle.

Propelled by a demonic case of diarrhea, the Yark shoots through the forest like a skyrocket.

At each stride, the poor wretch composes a symphony of farts. As he goes by, animals start up in surprise, afraid that the explosive reports signal the start of hunting season.

A mighty eruption launches him off the ground. Like a space rocket, he takes off straight into the sky. His gas-propelled bottom shoots him through the sound barrier. And like Pegasus, the Yark disappears amongst the stars, at full throttle.

Sick of his life, of himself, and of this loveless world,

the Yark wishes for only one thing: to dissolve into space for eternity.

As if to grant his wish, death appears before him. It takes the form of a chasm of light, a cool, glittering sun, a nuclear whiteness. The supersonic Yark hurtles into this fiery bowl with an explosion of shattering glass.

This spectacular shock, however, is by no means fatal. It's not in the afterlife that the Yark has run aground. He has crashed into the lantern of a lighthouse.

8

MADELEINE

No matter how long the night, it passes. A few days later, the Yark wakes up in a snug bed, tucked under a quilt of handsome purple velvet.

Sitting at his bedside, a child watches him. Silently, the Yark sniffs at this little girl with her big juicy eyes, her almond-scented skin and sugary breath.

"Where do you come from?" she asks. "What happened to you?"

"Poisoned," the beast replies in a whisper.

Little by little, his spirits revive, and the Yark looks around him.

His bed is in the middle of a round room with glass

walls. Around the windows, clouds coil like languid ghosts. You'd think that the room was floating in the air.

"Where am I?" the Monster stammers.

"In an abandoned lighthouse. This is where I live," the little girl murmurs, slipping a handful of herbs into the convalescent's mouth.

"And what's this?" the Monster asks in surprise.

"Mint, basil, and chamomile... All you need to cure a sore tummy."

This is the first time the Monster has ever tasted such a salad. But in the presence of so much innocence, he dares not say a word, and he munches in silence.

"My name's Madeleine. What's yours?"

Clearly, the little girl doesn't realize that he is a Monster. The Monster in question decides it's pointless to inform her of the fact and pretends to go back to sleep. He discreetly sniffs at the little girl to find out more about her, and he isolates her three main olfactory components. Violet and anise are the heart notes that reveal an underlying melancholy. The base notes of cotton and fresh rice attest to her goodness. Last, the Monster discerns a blend of blood orange and milk sugar, top notes that emanate only from the purest souls.

Moved to tears, the Yark wonders at this combination, which proves her to be the most wonderful little girl in the world.

"Poor little innocent!" he muses, choking back his saliva and his shame. "This angel has no idea that she's saved a demon! Ah, if she only knew the risk she runs in being so kind to me!"

A murmur from Madeleine interrupts his thoughts: "I thought you'd never wake up!"

Then she adds with a smile: "You gave me a scare, you know."

This is hardly the first time the Yark has scared someone. Fear of the Yark is to be expected. But Madeleine's fear is quite different.

He thinks her fear is *for him*.

"For me," the Monster repeats to himself in disbelief, for this is first time he's received such a feeling as a gift. At that, a wave of emotion sweeps over him. A sensation so new that he can't find a name for it.

After a lengthy silence, the Yark opens one eye.

"I don't frighten you?" he asks timidly.

"No!"

"You don't find me ugly?"

The little girl shrugs, as if the question is absurd.

"Actually, I find you beautiful!"

Beautiful? This word, which has never been used to describe him, gives him the shivers.

"Ordinarily, humans find me repulsive," the Monster whispers.

"Humans don't have a great deal of imagination. They see beauty only in what looks like them."

"But you're human yourself!" the Yark exclaims.

"True! And since I find you beautiful, that's proof that we look alike!"

With these few words, the little girl thinks she's said all she needs to. She smiles at the Monster, kisses him on the forehead, and leaves the room, wishing him good night.

The Yark finds himself alone with his exhaustion, the noise of the storm, and stirrings of happiness.

And now, he dreams... On an immense oval table, a constellation of dishes and bowls spreads out to infinity: boys in bacon, orphan gratin, chicken-fried children, breaded babies, leg of twins, brats in a bun, paté of little girl, stuffed schoolchildren, tandooried toddlers, choirboys in bundt cake...

But suddenly, a shock! The Yark discovers Madeleine's decapitated head lying on his plate. The child's big eyes stare sadly up at him. The Monster shrieks and wakes up in a cold sweat. For the first time in his life, a feast of children ends with a cry of horror!

9
TWO
FEELINGS

Although no scientific explanation can be given for it, the Yark and Madeleine became the best of friends in no time at all.

Their happiness, then, could have been perfect.

As perfect as galloping through the forest accompanied by wild creatures, soaring over ocean cliffs, and sweeping up into the sky to quench their thirst on clouds.

As perfect as those nights without speaking, or just spent laughing, nestled in the hollow of a shoulder, listening to another's heart beating.

Yes, everything could have been perfect.

But perfection is not of this world, and that happiness was soon to crumble away.

For the Monster was prey to two opposing feelings, two temptations so violent and contrary that they condemned his heart to torture.

Madeleine was so sweet and kind that he wanted with all his heart to cherish and protect her. Unfortunately, those very qualities also made him every bit as eager to eat her! He had to struggle relentlessly against himself, struggle against all he'd been since the dawn of time, struggle against the child-eating Monster that he was.

Ah, the dreadful dilemma! For the Yark would have preferred to die a thousand deaths than to hurt Madeleine.

The Yark resolved to subdue his instincts. No, his hunger would not triumph! No, his stomach would not dictate his fate! And for the ennobling of his soul, he told himself, art offered the ideal medium.

And so, the Yark became a painter.

His brush first sketched out lovely apples, handsome pears, then all of a sudden, DECAPITATED CHILDREN'S HEADS!

He immediately abandoned painting for sculpture. His chisel first carved out lovely spheres, handsome blocks, then all of a sudden, DECAPITATED CHILDREN'S HEADS!

He decided that pottery might suit him better. His fingers first shaped lovely vases, handsome bowls, then all of a sudden, DECAPITATED CHILDREN'S HEADS!

The Yark put an end to his artistic career by furiously trampling his leftover clay.

Seeing her friend downhearted, the little girl decides one evening to make him a dainty dessert.

"Here you are," she says, handing him a platter of buttery madeleines. The Monster lifts one of the tiny cakes to his trembling lips. The madeleine dissolves on his tongue and the Yark bursts into tears.

And so he confesses his terrible secret.

He tells Madeleine the extent of his shame. He tells her what a danger he is to her. He tells her he must leave. And he tells her how very frightened he's been of eating her!

A shudder runs through Madeleine. But it's not the threat of danger that makes her tremble. It's realizing all the love the Monster feels for her.

Distressed at the thought of him going away, she offers her hand to his jaws, without hesitation.

"Take a bite! Just a few fingers! I have plenty... Eat a few if it will calm your appetite!"

For a head-spinning moment, the Yark is tempted. But he gently folds the little pink hand and kisses it.

"Hunger is one form of suffering," he tells her. "But to hurt you would be a far worse one."

There. Everything has been said. Now the Yark must leave. When he opens the windows, Madeleine tries to hold him back.

"Don't leave me!"

The Monster pushes her away with a desperate growl.

"Are you really so eager to be eaten?"

In a single leap, he springs onto the roof and Madeleine implores him one last time.

"If you love me, stay..."

The Yark smiles sadly at her.

"You still don't understand? It's love that's making me leave you..."

He rises into the sky and, her eyes filled with tears, Madeleine watches her friend disappear amongst the stars.

Lost in space, the broken-hearted Monster lets himself fall. His sorrow weighs a thousand tons. He plummets like a rock, straight toward earth.

And he lands with a crash in the depths of the forest.

10
THE WILD
CHILDREN

T he birth of a baby is always an important event. The child's arrival into the benevolent world of people is rightly celebrated with cigars, champagne, and— for the lucky ones—the opening of a savings account.

But how fleeting is the golden age!

Because with the passing of the years, it becomes impossible not to admit that the child loses much of its charm. Physique and personality deteriorate with each birthday. Time thickens, disfigures, stupefies... And whose fault is that? It's the fault of the Beast that grows within the child, like a weed taking over a garden.

The age of reason marks the start of this spectacular deterioration. The faded cherub begins to ask questions, express ideas, and negotiate agendas. Capricious, gluttonous, and none too hygienic, the growing child's taste for raucous music and faddish clothing is an inconvenient and costly burden.

Yes, the golden age is fleeting!

And when cooing and baby talk have faded away, the parents are left with the prospect of a pimple-faced teenager.

Abandonment becomes necessary, in order to preserve pleasant memories. And so it is that a considerable number of children are abandoned every year in forests. In France alone, the number is estimated at sixty thousand. It is never with a light heart that parents hand over to Mother Nature the fate of their progeny. But they'll always find consolation in the resale of clothing and toys, a profit that will allow them to enjoy a few days of well-deserved rest and relaxation.

Lost in the depths of the forest and left to their own devices, these unfortunate wretches gradually return to their natural state. Far from school, they forget language and express themselves instead in rumbles and grunts of rage.

By observing them, we can get a basic idea of what humans were like at the dawn of our era: small starving bands in a permanent state of war, without faith, law, or toothbrushes, wandering the forest in search of fresh meat and blood.

This observation isn't of great interest because humanity has hardly evolved since the Iron Age.

Imagine the excitement of these wild children when they find the dying Yark on a path.

The snot oozing from their noses betrays their joy. This colossus will make a succulent treat! And what a windfall to satisfy their thirst for cruelty! Because the little beasts are well acquainted with the Yark's weakness. They know that their wickedness will keep the Monster from defending himself, much less from gobbling them up. The Yark denies their presence. The smell of these brats makes him nauseous. But, stunned by his fall, he's too weak to escape.

Like a thunderclap, the horde of children falls upon him. There are more than a hundred of them to bite, wrench, strangle, cling to his fangs, and yank on his wings, trying to tear them off. The Yark roars in pain.

"My time has come," he thinks, with a wave of sorrow and a hint of relief.

And so the huge hairy Monster stretches out on the ground to let them eat him raw. Certainly, he could shorten his ordeal by decapitating his diminutive

adversaries with a snap of his jaws. Their venomous flesh would kill him on the spot! But the tender-hearted Monster pities his assailants. Would they be so nasty if they hadn't been abandoned? Would they be so cruel if they had ever truly been loved? And then, the Yark thinks of all the children he's eaten. And as if to gain some smidgen of forgiveness, he finds it hardly unjust to be eaten in his turn.

But the wild children don't mean to finish off their prisoner right away. Even though they're famished—for weeks they've subsisted on spider droppings—their thirst for cruelty is more intense than their hunger.

The Yark is tied upside down to a tree trunk and the little beasts dance around their prisoner with blood-curdling cries.

A little redheaded boy, as skinny as a nail, approaches the Monster. He yanks a few hairs from his own head and stuffs them into the Yark's mouth. The colossus utters a hideous cry. This wisp from a naughty child burns like a white-hot needle. Amused by the spectacle, the children burst out laughing.

Then, taking turns in front of the Monster, they thrust down his throat small portions of their bodies: knee scabs, torn-off toenails, nose boogers, and things like that...

The children are careful not to feed him more than minuscule doses of poison. It would be a waste to kill the

Yark straightaway. For a torture session to be fun, it must be drawn out!

All night, the infernal celebration goes on.

At the end of his strength, the Monster can no longer so much as groan. He tells himself that by dawn it will all be over.

"Only a few hours to go," he thinks, "before these noxious imps will have finished me off."

But as his strength leaves him, an image surges up before his eyes. Madeleine's face appears in all its loveliness. Her smile wipes away his suffering. Her memory stamps out his sorrow.

And so the Yark no longer dreads the hours that remain until dawn.

11
BREAKFAST

I t's daybreak. A ray of sunlight tickles the Monster's snout and makes him sneeze. He stretches, blinks, and yawns voluptuously. Suddenly, he sits bolt upright.

"What? I'm not dead?"

Dumbfounded to find himself alive, the Monster listens to the beating of his heart. By what miracle has he regained his strength? He breathes the morning air, fills his lungs... The Monster has never felt so fit in his life.

"How can this be?" he murmurs, thinking of all the poison he swallowed during the night.

Worn out by their night-long festivities, the wild children snore at his feet. The Yark sniffs at them. Their scent of leather, ear wax, and rotting olives repulses him.

However, this morning, something is different.

The smell of scoundrels is making his mouth water!

Baffled by this mystery, the Yark loosens his ties and kneels beside the children to get a better whiff.

"Yum, what a good smell of bad children," he purrs, as astonished as he is hungry.

His cherry-red tongue licks greedily over their tiny heads.

But a flicker of pity keeps him from biting. In their sleep, these little wretches seem so touching, so fragile... The gallant Monster asks himself again: "Would they be so nasty if they hadn't been abandoned? Would they be so cruel if they had truly been loved?"

"They certainly would!" he roars without further effort to work it out.

And he throws himself on the children and munches them down, every last one.

"One hundred and two bad kids!" the Yark exclaims triumphantly, since he has counted each mouthful. One hundred and two bad kids and not even a tummy ache! Nothing! Not a single side effect! One hundred and two bad kids and not even a stray fart!

Whereupon, the Yark breaks into a dance of joy. And in spite of his abundant breakfast, he's never felt so light!

12
AROUND THE
WORLD

When a gigantic finger taps delicately at the lighthouse windows, Madeleine's face lights up with an immense smile.

The little girl jumps onto the Yark's shoulders and the two of them celebrate their reunion with a series of loop-the-loops above the waves.

That evening, while sampling a jar of candied fruit, the Monster regales Madeleine with the account of his extraordinary adventure. He is certainly astonished to have survived his ordeal with the wild children. But he's even more amazed to have successfully digested them.

"Divine miracle!" the Yark proclaims.

To Madeleine, there's nothing supernatural about it. Citing the adage, "That which does not kill me can only make me stronger," she explains that those tiny doses of bad children acted like a vaccine. Instead of killing him, the small quantities of poison immunized him against the toxic flesh of the rascals.

The Yark doesn't understand much of that explanation, but he nevertheless smacks his lips at the conclusion: "So now I can stuff myself with all the children in the whole world!" he exclaims.

"Freedom would mean that you could live without eating anyone," the little girl replies.

"To live without eating?" the Monster yelps.

"To live without killing anyone!" Madeleine corrects him with a laugh.

"But it's in a Monster's nature to eat little children!" the Yark says indignantly.

"There's no law that says so," Madeleine replies. "There's only what each of us decides for ourselves."

"Well, I'm pretty sure I'll never change!"

"Really? Then, why haven't you eaten me?" Madeleine retorts in a mischievous tone.

Not knowing how to reply, the Yark says nothing.

After a moment's thought, he lifts his hand to his heart: "Don't worry! I'll only eat brats from now on. Only wild children growing up in the forest!"

But Madeleine doesn't care whether the Yark's meals are nice or naughty. What bothers her is the fact that in order to live, he has to kill another living being.

In his embarrassment, the Monster hastily promises: "All right then, I swear it...I'll never eat another child."

Liar!

Because that very night, after making sure that Madeleine is sleeping like a baby, this glutton flies out the window to test his limitless appetite on children all around the world.

From high in the sky, the Yark lets himself drop sharply to earth and he lands by chance in Morocco.

His sense of smell leads him to a small house from which a delicious smell emanates. His mouth watering in anticipation, he slides into the bedroom, laughing to himself.

"Hee-hee! Whether he's a good boy or an utter brat, I'll gulp him down in a single bite!"

But the Monster is startled when he sees the child in his bed. This little Moroccan boy could be mistaken for Madeleine! And even though he looks nothing like her, the Yark could nonetheless swear he's her twin!

The shock spoils his appetite, so he hurries out of the room and flies straight off to Southeast Asia.

With great strides, the Monster sails through rice paddies, cursing the mosquitoes as he goes. But never mind the bites. The Monster is running full speed toward an orphanage.

In the silent dormitory, he creeps between the rows of little beds. When a splinter pierces his bottom, the stoical Monster refrains from crying out. Still, when he leans over the children, he can't keep back a howl.

All these little Vietnamese children look like Madeleine!

"I'm losing my mind!" the Yark yelps, trembling.

He rubs his eyes as he runs from bed to bed, but the Yark sees in each face the one child he could never eat.

All night long, the Yark visits thousands of bedrooms across all the earth's continents. And even though he travels from Spain to Bulgaria, from India to the United States, all the children of the world seem to have taken Madeleine's features.

For a long time, the Monster thinks he is suffering from hallucinations. Then at last he admits that the love of a little girl has made him see the world differently.

Since that night, the Yark has never eaten another child.

13
HIS
STORY

The Yark and Madeleine still live at the top of the lighthouse. Far from the rest of the world, they look after each other and lead a pleasant, secluded existence. And when the Monster wields his paintbrushes, these days he creates magnificent works of art.

Sometimes, the taste of children comes back to him and he recalls the feeding frenzies of days gone by. Then, when Madeleine is asleep, the Yark leaps onto the roof and vanishes into the night.

If you look up, you might see him gliding over the rooftops.

But don't be frightened. The Yark is no longer led by the nose. He flies with his eyes wide open.

Sometimes his gaze is drawn to the lighted window of a bedroom. And even if it's no more than a candle flame, the Yark sees it as a distress flare, a lighthouse in the night, the signal of a nightmare that's woken a child in its bed.

That is when the Monster descends to the earth.

His hooked nails open the front door. He creeps along the hallway and climbs the stairs without a sound.

Stalking like a silent wolf, he squeezes into the bedroom. His hand slides lightly over the wall to switch off the light. As he approaches the bed, he catches a whiff of a child terrified of the dark.

And to help the child go back to sleep, the Yark tells his story.

THE END

Acknowledgments

Nathalie Palméro, Julien Messemackers,
François Tessier & Valéria Vanguelov.

This edition first published in 2018 by Gecko Press
PO Box 9335, Wellington 6141, New Zealand
info@geckopress.com

English-language edition © Gecko Press Ltd 2018

Translation © Antony Shugaar 2018

Original title: *Le Yark* © 2011 Éditions Grasset & Fasquelle
Text © Bertrand Santini
Illustrations © Laurent Gapaillard

Distribution
United States and Canada:
Lerner Publishing Group, lernerbooks.com
United Kingdom: Bounce Sales and Marketing, bouncemarketing.co.uk
Australia: Scholastic Australia, scholastic.com.au
New Zealand: Upstart Distribution, upstartpress.co.nz

Edited by Penelope Todd
Design and typesetting by Katrina Duncan
Printed in China by Everbest Printing Co Ltd,
an accredited ISO 14001 & FSC certified printer

ISBN hardback: 978-1-776571-71-0 (USA)
ISBN paperback: 978-1-776571-72-7
Ebook available

For more curiously good books, visit geckopress.com